Dear Parents,

Welcome to the Scholastic Reader series. We have taken over 80 years of experience with teachers, parents, and children and put it into a program that is designed to match your child's interests and skills.

Level 1—Short sentences and stories made up of words kids can sound out using their phonics skills and words that are important to remember.

Level 2—Longer sentences and stories with words kids need to know and new "big" words that they will want to know.

Level 3—From sentences to paragraphs to longer stories, these books have large "chunks" of texts and are made up of a rich vocabulary.

Level 4—First chapter books with more words and fewer pictures.

It is important that children learn to read well enough to succeed in school and beyond. Here are ideas for reading this book with your child:

- Look at the book together. Encourage your child to read the title and make a prediction about the story.
- Read the book together. Encourage your child to sound out words when appropriate. When your child struggles, you can help by providing the word.
- Encourage your child to retell the story. This is a great way to check for comprehension.
- Have your child take the fluency test on the last page to check progress.

Scholastic Readers are designed to support your child's efforts to learn how to read at every age and every stage. Enjoy helping your child learn to read and love to read.

—**Francie Alexander**
Chief Education Officer
Scholastic Education

To Super-Tutor Rosemary Hall
—K.M.

To Wills and Georgia
—M.S.

Library of Congress Cataloging-in-Publication Data is available.

ISBN: 0-590-03269-0

10 9 8 7 6 5 4 3 2 1 03 04 05 06 07
Printed in the U.S.A. 23 • First printing, April 1998

by **Kate McMullan**

Illustrated by **Mavis Smith**

Scholastic Reader — Level 3

SCHOLASTIC INC.

New York Toronto London Auckland Sydney
Mexico City New Delhi Hong Kong Buenos Aires

Fluffy the Hero

Fluffy went home with Maxwell
for summer vacation.
Oh, boy! thought Fluffy.
I will nibble grass.
I will lie in the sun.
I love summer!

Maxwell put Fluffy's cage in the den.
He gave Fluffy seeds and water.
"I'm going to the park,"
Maxwell told Fluffy.
"I will see you later!"
Wait! thought Fluffy. **What will *I* do?**

Maxwell's sister, Violet,
came into the den.
"Are you tired of being in that cage?"
she asked Fluffy.
You got that right, thought Fluffy.
"Do you want to go outside with me?"
asked Violet.
Do I ever! thought Fluffy.
Take me to the grass!

Violet picked Fluffy up.
"I'm going to take you swimming,"
she said.
Take me WHAT? thought Fluffy.

Hey! Stop! Wait a second!
thought Fluffy. **I am a land animal!**
I walk. I run. I even trot.
But I do NOT swim!

Violet carried Fluffy outside
to her wading pool.
She put him on the back of a yellow duck.
She pushed the duck
toward the middle of the pool.
"Whee!" she said.

The duck bounced up and down.
Fluffy held onto the duck's neck.
Easy, big fellow, he said to the duck.
I don't want to get wet!

Violet jumped into the wading pool.

“Isn’t this fun?” she said.

Not yet, thought Fluffy.

Violet kicked and splashed.

“Whee!” she said.

The duck bounced up and down.

Stop! thought Fluffy. **Whoa, Duckie!**

Then Fluffy saw a fin in the water.
A shark was swimming toward Violet!
Fluffy had to save her!

Go! Go! Go! Fluffy called to his duck.
Fluffy rode toward the shark.
Faster! he called to his duck.

The duck carried Fluffy
over to the shark.
Fluffy hit the shark on the head.
He popped it in the nose.
Fluffy hit him again, right in the teeth!
That did it.
The shark rolled over.

Fluffy the Hero rode his duck
over to Violet.
You are safe now, Violet, thought Fluffy.
That shark will not hurt you.

Violet picked Fluffy up.
No, no, do not thank me,
thought Fluffy the Hero.
I was only doing my job.

Violet dunked Fluffy in the water.

"Whee!" she cried.

A hero's life is never easy,

thought Fluffy.

A Prize for Fluffy

Maxwell, Wade, and Emma
read a sign in a pet shop window.
It said:

"Fluffy could win a prize," Emma said.

***A* prize?** thought Fluffy.

I'll win ALL the prizes!

On Saturday morning,
Emma washed Fluffy's face and ears.
Maxwell washed Fluffy's paws.
Wade turned him over
and washed his tummy.

Enough! thought Fluffy.

I'm not going for the CLEAN prize!

EST
ETS
TEST

“We want to enter Fluffy
in the contest,” Maxwell told Mr. Small.
You are looking at the big winner!
thought Fluffy.
Mr. Small wrote down Fluffy’s name.

All kinds of pets came for the contest.
But there was only one other guinea pig.
Maxwell put Fluffy down beside it.
I am a crested pig,
the other guinea pig told Fluffy.
She scratched her head. **I am going to win this contest.**

Fluffy's eyes got very big.

The other guinea pig was Kiss!

Kiss did not seem to remember Fluffy.

But Fluffy remembered her.

Kiss had eaten his valentine apple.

Kiss had said his toys were junk.

Fluffy did not like Kiss.

I am beautiful, Kiss told Fluffy.

I am smart. I can do a million tricks.

I will win all the prizes.

I don't think so, said Fluffy.

BEST
PETS
CONTEST

“Kiss!” called Mr. Small.

A girl took Kiss onto the stage.

Kiss turned around.

Kiss counted to one.

Kiss rolled over.

Fluffy thought Kiss was very good.

He bit his nails.

Can I beat her? he wondered.

Did you see me? Kiss asked when her turn was over. **I was really great, wasn't I?**

Kiss scratched her head again.
Fluffy saw some dark spots on her crest.
Kiss had fleas!
One of her fleas jumped onto Fluffy.
Yikes! thought Fluffy.

"Fluffy!" called Mr. Small.

Maxwell carried Fluffy onto the stage.

He put Fluffy down.

Fluffy shook his head.

He shook his arms and his legs.

He had to get that flea off!

Fluffy skipped across the stage.
“Go, Fluffy!” called Wade.

Fluffy turned upside down
and kicked his feet.
“What a pig!” called Emma.

Fluffy scratched his head with one paw.
He rubbed his tummy with the other.
He had to get rid of that flea!
The flea was on Fluffy's head.
All of Fluffy's jumping around had
made the flea very dizzy.
The flea jumped off Fluffy.
Yes! thought Fluffy.
The flea was gone!
He pumped his paw in the air as he
ran off stage.

"Here is a prize," said Mr. Small.
"It is for the best dancer...Fluffy!"
Everyone clapped and clapped.

"Wow," Maxwell said.
"How did Fluffy
get to be such a good dancer?"
I think I will keep that a secret,
thought Fluffy.

Big, Bad Fluffy

Maxwell took Fluffy out to the backyard.
Fluffy looked around.
It's a jungle out here! he thought.
"Keep an eye on Fluffy, Maxwell,"
said his mom.
"Don't worry," said Maxwell.
"Fluffy won't go anywhere."

Maxwell lay down in the backyard.
He put Fluffy down next to him.
Maxwell watched Fluffy nibble grass.
He watched him sniff the ground.
Maxwell closed his eyes.
Fluffy wandered away.

In the jungle, thought Fluffy,
danger is everywhere.

Fluffy walked into the jungle.
A lion poked his head out of the brush.
Get back! thought Fluffy.
**You do NOT want to mess
with a big, bad pig!**
The lion ran back into the brush.

Fluffy made his way through the jungle.

A snake lay in his path.

Go away! thought Fluffy.

Or I will tie you in a big, bad knot!

The snake crawled off.

Fluffy walked deeper into the jungle.
A tiger jumped out at him.

You don't scare me! thought Fluffy.
I'm big! And I'm bad!
The tiger hurried away.

Fluffy smiled.
It is good to be big and bad,
he thought.

Suddenly a dog barked at Fluffy.
Fluffy jumped! He started running.
He saw a hole at the bottom of a tree.
He dove into it to hide.

But the hole was not empty.
It was full of baby rabbits.

Fluffy saw the dog
running for the rabbit hole.
Fluffy jumped into the nest
of baby rabbits.

The dog stuck its head
into the rabbit hole.
Fluffy tried to look
like a cute little bunny.

The dog went away.
Sometimes, thought Fluffy,
it is good to be little and cute.

Just then, Mama Rabbit came home.
Mama Rabbit picked up
one of her babies.
She picked up another one.
She bent down to pick up Fluffy.
Uh oh, thought Fluffy.

You are not one of my babies!
Mama Rabbit said.
She growled at Fluffy.
Get out of my nest
or you will be sorry!

Fluffy leaped out of the nest.
He jumped out of the rabbit hole.
He ran across the backyard
straight to Maxwell.

Maxwell opened his eyes.
"I knew you would not go anywhere,"
he said to Fluffy.
Maxwell picked Fluffy up and took him
inside.

Sometimes, thought Fluffy,
it is good to be home.